THE UNOFFICIAL

◄◄◄ MINECRAFT™ TOOL KIT ►►►

RIDE THE WAVES

WITH MINECRAFT™

JOEY DAVEY   JONATHAN GREEN   JULIET STANLEY

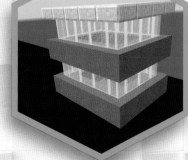

Gareth Stevens
PUBLISHING

Please visit our website, **www.garethstevens.com**.
For a free color catalog of all our high-quality books,
call toll free 1-800-542-2595 or fax 1-877-542-2596.

Cataloging-in-Publication Data

Names: Davey, Joey. | Green, Jonathan. | Stanley, Juliet.
Title: Ride the waves with Minecraft™ / Joey Davey, Jonathan Green, and Juliet Stanley.
Description: New York : Gareth Stevens Publishing, 2018. |
Series: The unofficial Minecraft™ tool kit | Includes index.
Identifiers: LCCN ISBN 9781538217146 (pbk.) | ISBN 9781538217092 (library bound) |
ISBN 9781538217047 (6 pack)
Subjects: LCSH: Minecraft (Game)--Juvenile literature. | Minecraft (Video game)--
Handbooks, manuals, etc.--Juvenile literature. |
Classification: LCC GV1469.M55 D38 2018 | DDC 794.8--dc23

Published in 2018 by
Gareth Stevens Publishing
111 East 14th Street, Suite 349
New York, NY 10003

Designed and packaged by: Dynamo Limited
Built and written by: Joey Davey, Jonathan Green, and Juliet Stanley

Printed in the United States of America
CPSIA compliance information: Batch CW18GS: For further information contact
Gareth Stevens, New York, New York at 1-800-542-2595.

CONTENTS

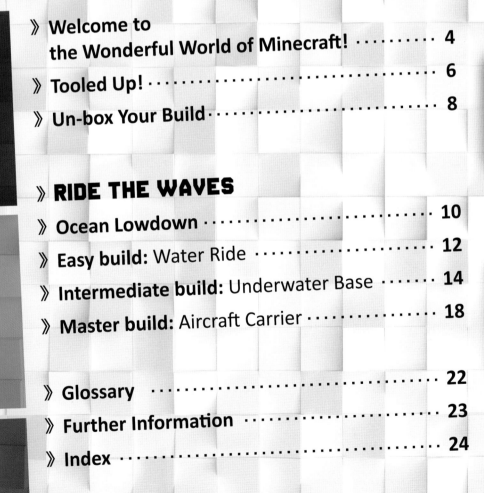

WELCOME
TO THE WONDERFUL WORLD OF
MINECRAFT!

If you're reading this, then you're probably already familiar with the fantastic game of building blocks and going on adventures. If you're not, go download Minecraft now and try it out!

Courtesy of IAmNewAsWell

READY?

OKAY, LET'S GET STARTED!

« THE AIM OF THE GAME »

This book has projects of three different difficulty ratings, which will help you hone your building skills. Each project has clear step-by-step instructions. You'll also find expert tips, like this one . . .

One of the greatest things about Minecraft – apart from being able to explore randomly generated worlds – is that you can build amazing things, from the simplest home to the grandest castle. This book will help you become a master builder, capable of building your own epic Minecraft masterpieces.

EXPERT TIP!

CREATIVE MODE vs SURVIVAL MODE

If you build in Creative mode, you'll have all the blocks you need to complete your build, no matter how outlandish. However, if you like more of a challenge, why not build in Survival mode? Just remember – you'll have to mine all your resources first, and you will also be kept busy crafting weapons and armor to fend off dangerous mobs of zombies and creepers!

Courtesy of crpeh

FAIL TO PREPARE AND PREPARE TO FAIL

If you're building in Survival mode, before you get going, you'll need to set up your hotbar so that items such as torches, tools, and weapons are all within easy reach. You'll also want to make sure that you're building on a flat surface.

For the best results, use Minecraft PC to complete all of the step-by-step builds in this book.

Before you start, you'll need to mine all your resources, and before you can do that, you'll need to sort out your Tool Kit . . . turn the page for further help.

Courtesy of swifsampson

EXPERT TIP!

ALL THAT GLITTERS

If you're planning on creating a Minecraft masterpiece, you'll want some super-special materials. To find rare ores, like diamonds, mine a staircase to Level 14 and then strip-mine the area. But remember – you'll need an iron or diamond pickaxe to mine most ores. If you use any other type of tool, you'll destroy the block without getting anything from it.

Courtesy of Cornbass

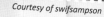

STAYING SAFE ONLINE

Minecraft is one of the most popular games in the world, and you should have fun while you're playing it. However, it is just as important to stay safe when you're online.

Top tips for staying safe are:
» turn off chat
» find a kid-friendly server
» watch out for viruses and malware
» set a game-play time limit
» tell a trusted adult what you're doing

TOOLED UP!

Before you get cracking – or should that be crafting? – you're going to need to make sure that you're set with all the tools you'll need.

≪ CUSTOMIZE YOUR HOTBAR ≫

Your inventory is the place where everything you mine and collect is stored. You can access it at any time during the game.

When you exit your inventory, a hotbar will appear at the bottom of the screen, made up of a line of nine hotkey slots. Think of this as your mini-inventory where you can keep the things you use most frequently.

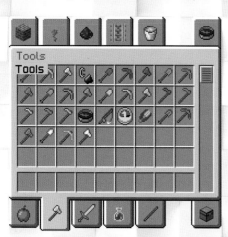

It's vitally important to take time to organize your hotbar carefully – in a game of Survival, it might just save your life!

Move an item from your inventory into one of the hotkey slots to assign it. Then, when you select a slot, the item you have placed in there will automatically appear in your hand, ready for you to use.

≪ HOT OR NOT ≫

Always keep at least one weapon and one food source in your hotbar. Also make sure you've got some tools in there. It's always handy to have a pickaxe or two, or perhaps a shovel, depending on what you're planning on mining. A torch will also be handy. Last of all, you want to make sure that you have some basic building materials ready.

GO FISH!

EXPERT TIP!

Fishing rods are surprisingly useful. You can use them to catch fish, and you can also cast them to set off pressure plates while you stay out of harm's way.

≪ BUILDING BLOCKS ≫

EXPERT TIP!

WOOD

Always useful, as you need it to craft many everyday items. In Survival mode, always carry some logs with you – especially if you're going caving, as wood is hard to find underground.

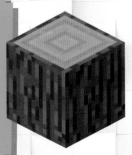

REDSTONE RAMPAGE

If you want your Minecraft masterpiece to have moving mechanisms, like a roller coaster, you're going to need some redstone. This block allows you to create moving parts, and even circuits.

STONE

The most common block in the game, it is good at keeping creepers at bay. If you're planning on building a castle, stone is what you're going to need – and lots of it!

OBSIDIAN

Other than bedrock, this is the hardest material – and it's completely creeper-proof! You'll need an entire lava source block and 15 seconds with a diamond pick to mine it in Survival mode, though.

BRICK

Harder than stone and can be crafted out of clay, although it does take a long time to craft and will drain your fuel supply.

≪ MIND-BOGGLING ≫ BIOMES

The different types of terrain you encounter in Minecraft are called biomes. They range from ice plains and swamps, to deserts and jungles, to oceans and fantasy islands.

Courtesy of MADbakamono

Courtesy of Epic Minecraft Seeds

These biomes will take you to the sky and back, quite literally!

UN-BOX YOUR BUILD

The amazing world of Minecraft is made from lots and lots of . . . blocks! But these simple, straight-edged blocks certainly don't stop its biggest fans from building masterpieces that curve, spiral, and defy the cuboid. With a little help and a lot of imagination, you can make even your wildest dream builds come true. Let's take a look at some of the creative possibilities Minecraft has to offer.

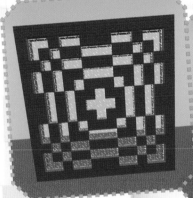

« ECCENTRIC ENTRANCES »

Make your entrances unforgettable with lots of different materials, shapes, and a few surprises! The first door is the perfect entrance for a treetop lodge. From a distance it looks like it has been carved out of a tree trunk by woodland creatures. There's a hidden entrance in the second doorway, and the colors created by wool and emerald blocks are totally wild!

« WOW FACTOR WINDOWS »

Why not try your hand at making these stunning windows? Short rows, L-shapes, and single blocks create a circular web within the frame of the first window. Diagonally placed blocks in the second window create curved lines that look like a propeller. But you don't have to stick to square windows – anything is possible in Minecraft!

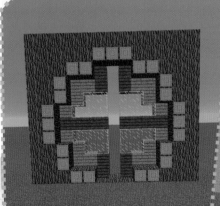

EXPERT TIP!

SKETCH IT

Being prepared will make building in Minecraft easier and much more fun. You'll have a good idea of what you want your final build to look like, and you'll have given yourself time to think about how to do it. Forget math for a second – grid paper is perfect for planning what to do with all of these blocks!

The dark blue flooring and back wall cleverly disguise this open entrance.

≪ REMARKABLE ≫ ROOFS

Here are three in-spire-ational roofs for you to try! For a look inspired by ancient Chinese architecture, add blocks in the corners of simple roof structures. Or go for a space age design with lava, emerald, diamond, and beacon blocks! Staying hidden is always a good strategy in Survival mode – this last grass roof is the perfect way to disguise your builds.

≪ SENSATIONAL ≫ STRUCTURES

Yes, it's a woolly hat house made from wool blocks! Try recreating this circular structure with lots of different-sized rows. The only rule is: stay symmetrical. This arched bridge is a super-simple structure, and it can be used to add interest to the front of a building, or to un-box square windows. The last building uses columns to support a balcony and to add texture to its surface. This would be a great look for a castle.

EXPERT TIP!

BE INSPIRED

Search online or flip through books to find inspiration for your creations! As well as a myriad of Minecraft buildings, you'll find plenty of weird and wonderful real-life buildings that you can use to help you come up with your very own masterpiece. Happy building, Minecrafters!

OCEAN LOWDOWN

Magnificent octopus?

No! Magnum opus! It means "great work."

You know where you'll find some of the most awesome builds in Minecraft? Under the sea! So why not take the plunge and craft your own underwater magnum opus?

《 BUILDING UNDERWATER 》

《 MOSTLY WATER 》

Around 60% of the Overworld's surface is covered by ocean, so there's plenty of space to build your own awesome underwater habitat. In Deep Ocean biomes, the sea can exceed 30 blocks in depth. The ground is mainly covered with gravel and ocean monuments. Guardians spawn there. These attack with lasers and drop raw fish and prismarine when defeated.

The most efficient way to build underwater in Survival mode is to follow these simple steps:

》 Swim to the bottom of the sea with as much wood as you can.

》 Using the wood, build a dome-shaped frame on the seafloor.

》 Cover the frame in a layer of glass.

》 Dig through the seabed, under the edge of your build, and then dig up again underneath it. This will create an air pocket.

》 Using flint and iron, set fire to the wooden frame.

》 When the wood has burned away, you will be left with a hollow, pressurized glass dome.

EXPERT TIP!

BREATHE EASY

If you want to build an underwater colony in Survival mode, create a series of work shelters around your construction site. These will trap air pockets, so you can catch your breath without having to swim to the surface. Just make sure that they are no further apart than the distance you can travel on one lungful of air.

≪ PRISMARINE DREAM ≫

Prismarine is a stone-like material that only appears underwater in ocean monuments. It can be mined using any pickaxe. Four prismarine shards will craft one block of prismarine, nine prismarine shards will craft one prismarine brick, while eight prismarine shards and one ink sac will make one block of dark prismarine.

Prismarine is both decorative and highly blast resistant. Normal prismarine is unique in that it has an animated texture – the cracks in its surface slowly change color from aqua, to green, to purple, to indigo, and back again.

EXPERT TIP!

SQUIDS IN

Squid are eight-legged mobs that spawn in water (which can include your swimming pool and not just ocean and rivers). They are always passive. If killed, they drop between one and three ink sacs, which can be used to dye wool and prismarine, and make books.

Collecting ink sacs can be time-consuming, so why not set up a squid farm? Under the sea, the best way to do this is to dig a funnel underneath the ocean. (If you're on land, either craft a lake, or find a shallow pre-existing one.)

WATER RIDE »

**DIFFICULTY
EASY**

**TIME
1 HOUR**

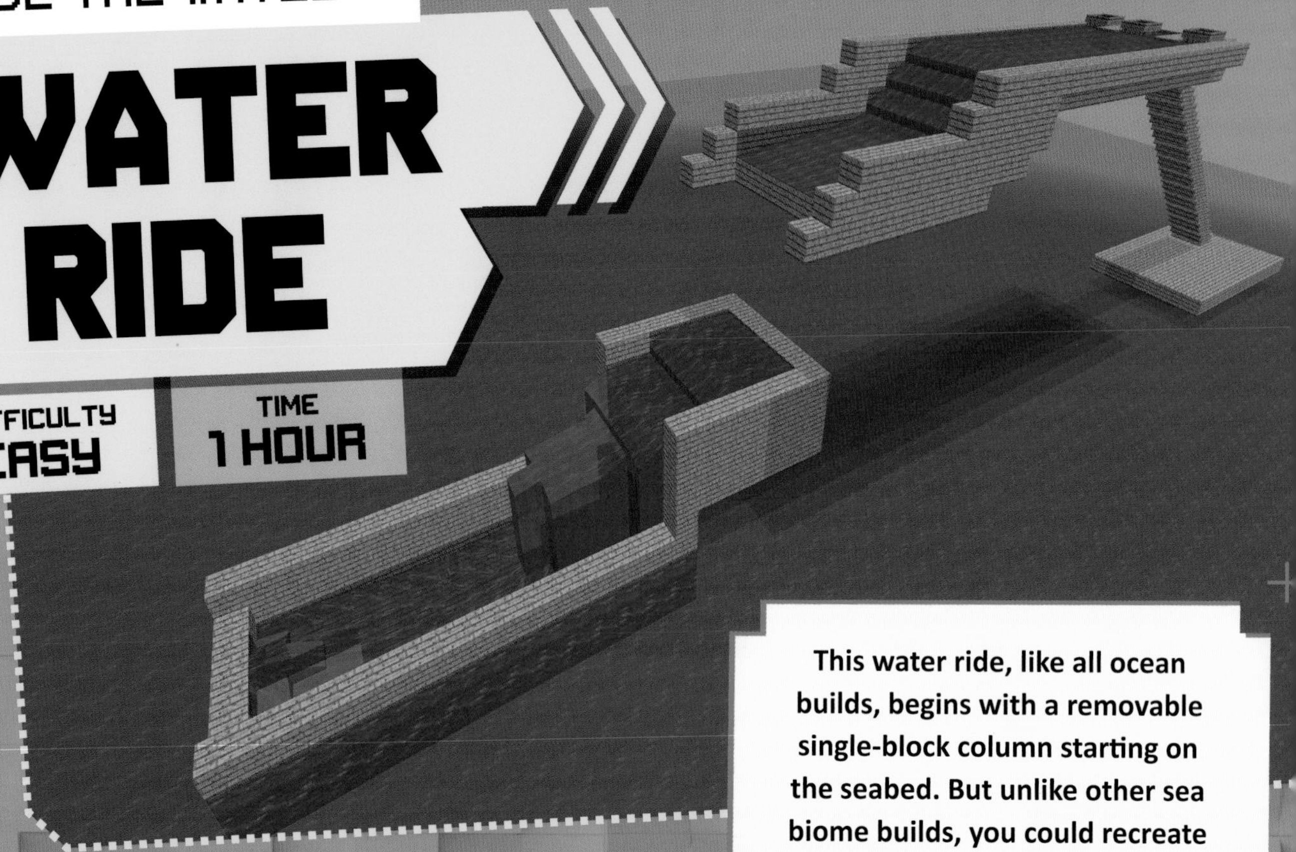

This water ride, like all ocean builds, begins with a removable single-block column starting on the seabed. But unlike other sea biome builds, you could recreate this ride on land if you want to make a fantastic theme park!

MATERIALS

STEP 1

Create an oak-wood-plank platform on the surface of the sea. Build your stairway from oak wood stair. Make it 14 blocks high. Each step should be constructed from four blocks and be two blocks wide, as shown.

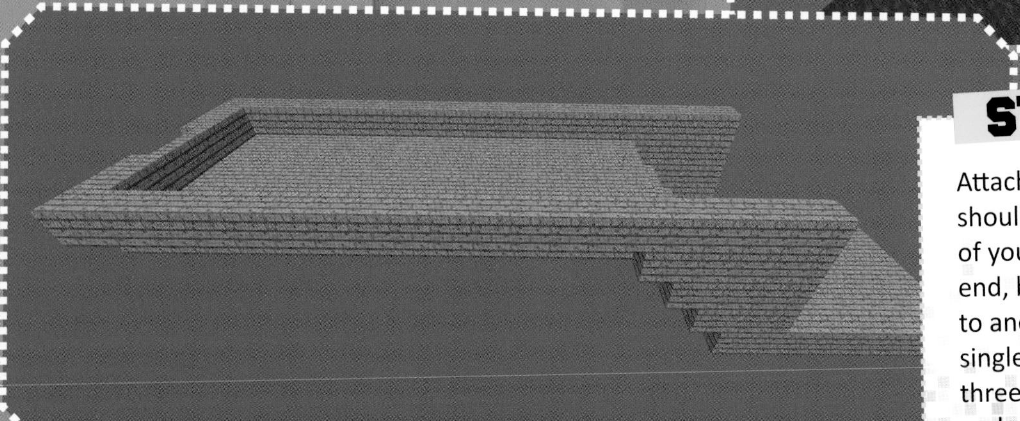

STEP 2

Attach a platform (6x15 blocks should work well) to one end of your stairway. At the other end, build two steps down to another platform. Place single-block rows around three sides of the upper level and steps, as shown.

STEP 3

Extend the walls down the steps and along the lower platform. They will contain the water before it plunges down to the second part of the ride.

STEP 4

Build two three-oak-wood-plank rows at the start of your ride so passengers can climb aboard. Find three boats in your inventory and add those too. Then just find a water bucket and add water!

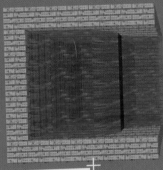

STEP 5

Five blocks below the first part of your ride, make a cube with the top and front missing. To get the water flowing, add a row of blocks along the back of the cube. Tap under each with a water bucket to make the water flow evenly, then remove this row of blocks.

STEP 6

To create a dizzying drop, add more blocks under the front of your cube, as shown. Attach these to a 7x16x3-block hollow cuboid without its top. This cuboid will form the end of your water ride.

WATER LEVELS

EXPERT TIP!

Add as many levels as you want to make this ride longer. Simply raise your steps and repeat the build for the platform you have already created. Also, you can craft twists and turns by losing the straight lines and staggering your blocks as you build.

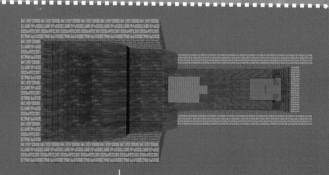

STEP 7

Remove 3x3 blocks from the base of the last part of your ride – this is the ride exit. Add 13 blocks (shown here in green) to the bottom of your cube between the two levels to help the water flow. Once the water is flowing nicely, you can remove these blocks.

UNDERWATER BASE

DIFFICULTY
INTERMEDIATE

BUILD TIME
2 HOURS

Now that your Minecrafting skills are reaching awesome heights, it's time to move in a different direction – under the waves! For this build, you are going to create a secret hideout under the sea that is out of this world. There's plenty of room to make this your own with a massive interior that you can turn into a control center, crafting studio or stylish home.

MATERIALS

STEP 1

Build the walls of your underwater base from iron block. Build a shape like the one shown. Make it four blocks high with two layers below the waterline and two above.

STEP 2

Add another three layers under the waterline so the walls are seven blocks high. Use sponge blocks to empty the water from the area inside the walls. You'll need to empty one layer of water blocks at a time.

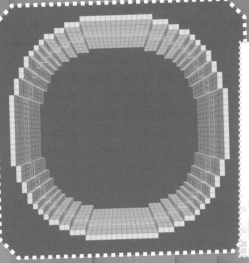

STEP 3

For your roof support, build a ring of glass blocks around the inside of your walls, three blocks down from the top, as shown. Then add another smaller ring of glass blocks one block above to create a step up.

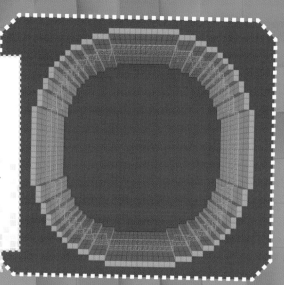

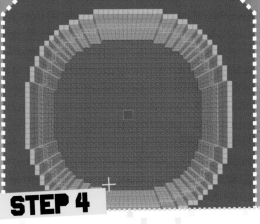

STEP 4

Now add the roof. Build a circle slightly smaller than the second ring to form a glass dome for the best view and maximum light. Leave four blocks open in the center to help you position the next stage of your build.

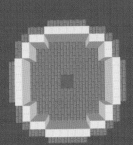

STEP 5

Build a stone-brick-block base on top of your glass roof with a four-block hole in the center that sits on the hole in the glass roof. Build nine-block-high quartz walls, two blocks in from the edges. Remove the two iron-block rows above the waterline from the outer ring.

STEP 6

Five blocks up from the brick base, build a stone-brick-stair ledge around your tower. Add windows by replacing four quartz blocks with gray stained glass on each long side. Then build another ledge above your windows with two rows of stone brick stair.

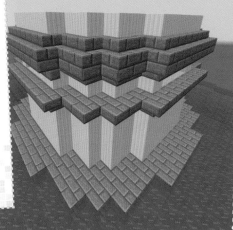

EXPERT TIP!

SUBMARINE DREAM

Make your underwater space even more spectacular with additional lighting, furniture, and canvases. You can even section off areas to make a series of rooms.

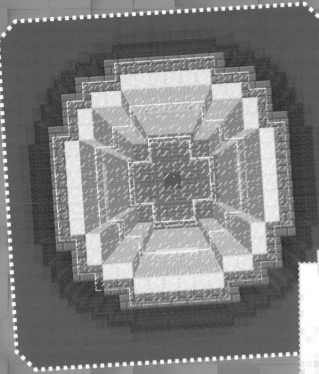

STEP 7

Build your roof from three two-block-wide tiers of glass. The first tier should follow the edges of the walls. The second tier should be smaller than the first and the third should form a cross. Then add one more stone-brick-stair ledge above the last one, as shown.

STEP 8

Now it's time to add to the underwater part of your build. Remove some glass-block squares under your entrance tower floor as shown to reveal the brickwork above. Add three more layers to the bottom of your walls, removing water as you go. Build an iron block floor and place glowstone columns around your walls to light your underwater interior.

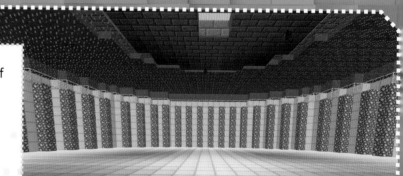

STEP 9

On the ceiling, fill the space where you removed the glass in the previous step with iron-block squares. Then create a smaller stone-brick-block layer underneath it. Build a 3x3-glowstone square around the central hole and add water for the lift.

STEP 10

On the top floor of your entrance tower place a glowstone block in each corner between the walls and the glass roof. Build a stone-brick floor with a 2x2-block hole in the center and add water to the center of your roof to continue your lift.

STEP 11

One floor down, build stone brick stair around the edges of your floor for decoration. Add glowstone blocks for lighting to each corner and around the edge of the 2x2-block gap in the center of the ceiling. Water will flow from above.

EXPERT TIP!

DEEP DOWN

Using your newfound knowledge, build lower chambers with glass sides so you can see everything that's happening under the sea and link them up with water lifts.

STEP 12

Create an entrance by removing 3x2 blocks from the wall. Add two blocks to the front of your base, topped with cobblestone wall and torches. These will form jetties for your boats. Now your underwater base is complete!

RIDE THE WAVES

AIRCRAFT CARRIER

Create a build that puts you on top of the watery world! You can land mod planes here and it provides the perfect base for some awesome underwater exploration. What's more, you might become host to some very special creatures – bats love the dark space provided inside this build.

DIFFICULTY MASTER

BUILD TIME 3 HOURS +

MATERIALS

STEP 1

Build a 50x15 red-hardened-clay base on the ocean surface. At one end, remove 19 blocks from either side (shown here in green). Then add eight more blocks (also shown in green) to create the front end of the aircraft carrier.

STEP 2

Next, add 45 blocks of red hardened clay to create the back of the aircraft carrier's base – these are shown in green here to help you.

18

STEP 3

Build a one-block-high wall around the edge of your base in cyan hardened clay.

STEP 4

Make your walls one block higher, then add a three-block row of cyan hardened clay (shown in green) at one end to create the ship's prow. Strengthen the back of the boat with more cyan hardened clay (also shown in green).

STEP 5

Build the walls of the aircraft carrier two blocks higher. Then remove the lowest row of blocks from the back of the aircraft carrier so the very end is above the waterline and add six more blocks, as shown in green.

EXPERT TIP!

MOD ALERT!

You may want to download a plane mod for this build. When looking for mods, always search for the "most viewed" ones and watch YouTube clips of mods with thousands of views. These are likely to be tried, tested, and safe to use. Also, save your Minecraft world before you introduce a mod. That way, if there's a problem, you can restore everything and start again!

STEP 6

Remove the blocks highlighted in green. This is in preparation for building your aircraft carrier downwards, below the waterline.

Build a line of red hardened clay one block below your red-hardened-clay base (shown in green). Then build another row one block below that (shown in yellow).

STEP 8

On the same level, add another line of red hardened clay (shown in purple). Then, one block down from this, build your lowest level, also in red hardened clay (shown in blue).

STEP 9

Back on the surface, it's time to build your deck. Build a rim of black hardened clay around the top edge of your aircraft carrier and then build your deck on the same level (shown here in green) from more black hardened clay.

STEP 10

Now extend your deck with black hardened clay to create a runway, as shown here in green to help you.

STEP 11

Now for your command center . . . Build a 4x5 base from cyan hardened clay with one-block-high walls around the edges, as shown. Add a layer of gray stained glass, then clay, then glass and finally stone slab, as shown.

STEP 12

Add the finishing touches to your command center with a stone-slab column topped with four cobblestone torch holders, as pictured. Add more slabs to the roof, and top two of these with shorter cobblestone-wall torch holders.

STEP 13

Use glowstone, yellow, and cyan hardened clay blocks to craft your main runway and helipad, as shown. Remember to remove black hardened clay blocks before placing the new blocks so your runway surface stays flat.

STEP 14

Extend one side of your aircraft carrier using 64 black hardened clay blocks (shown in green).

STEP 15

For support underneath, add blocks between the side of the aircraft carrier and the deck (shown here in green).

STEP 16

Now create a second runway using torches and yellow hardened clay blocks. Again, remove black hardened clay blocks before placing these on your deck. Then extend the rear of your aircraft carrier as shown in green here.

STEP 17

Add torches to the deck's edges. Build a 17-stone-slab walkway one block above the waterline with iron bar along the side so you don't fall overboard. Create four three-block-wide openings, ready to let in your first passenger – a stowaway bat!

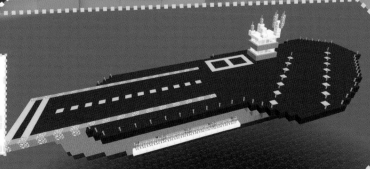

GLOSSARY

The world of Minecraft is one that comes with its own set of special words. Here are just some of them.

《 BIOME 》

A region in a Minecraft world with special geographical features, plants, and weather conditions. There are forest, jungle, desert, and snow biomes, and each one contains different resources and numbers of mobs.

《 COLUMN 》

A series of blocks placed on top of each other.

《 DIAGONAL 》

A line of blocks joined corner to corner that looks like a staircase.

《 HOTBAR 》

The selection bar at the bottom of the screen, where you put your most useful items for easy access during Survival mode.

《 INVENTORY 》

This is a pop-up menu containing tools, blocks and other Minecraft items.

《 MOB 》

Short for "mobile," a mob is a moving Minecraft creature with special behaviors. Villagers, animals, and monsters are all mobs, and they can be friendly, like sheep and pigs, or hostile, like creepers. All spawn or breed and some – like wolves and horses – are tamable.

《 MOD 》

Short for "modification," a mod is a piece of code that changes elements of the game.

《 ROW 》

A horizontal line of blocks.

FURTHER INFORMATION

BOOKS

Minecraft: Guide to Creative by Mojang AB and The Official Minecraft Team. Del Rey, 2017.

Minecraft: Guide to Exploration by Mojang AB and The Official Minecraft Team. Del Ray, 2017.

Minecraft: The Complete Handbook Collection by Stephanie Mitton and Paul Soares Jr. Scholastic, 2015.

WEBSITES

Visit the official Minecraft website to get started!
https://minecraft.net/en-us/

Explore over 600 kid-friendly Minecraft videos
at this awesome site!
https://www.cleanminecraftvideos.com

INDEX